Miles McHale, TATTLETALE

written by
CHRISTIANNE JONES

art by
ELINA ELLIS

First published in 2016 by Curious Fox,
an imprint of Capstone Global Library Limited,
264 Banbury Road, Oxford, OX2 7DY –
Registered company number: 6695582
www.curious-fox.com

ISBN 978 1 782 02608 2

20 19 18 17 16
10 9 8 7 6 5 4 3 2 1

A CIP catalogue for this book is available from the British Library.

Printed and bound in China.

Designed by Aruna Rangarajan

To Emma, Allie, Thomas, Nolan, Kale, Elsa,
Adalyn, and Landon. Don't be tattletales. — CJ

To my darling boy, Sasha Ellis. — Elina Ellis

Miles McHale was smart.
He was funny. He was sweet.

But Miles McHale was also a **TATTLETALE** –
and not just a one-or-two-times-a-day tattler.

Frank won't stop staring at me!

Hattie is going too fast!

We're talking about
CONSTANT
tattling, all day long.

That boy is picking his nose.

The tattling was a
problem at home.

But it was a BIG problem at school.

And Miles wasn't the only tattler.
(But he was the **worst** one.)
So one day, Mrs Snitcher started the
TATTLE BATTLE.

"Okay, class. The rules are simple:
two teams, one week, no tattling.

Whichever team has the fewest
number of tattles gets
EXTRA PLAYTIME on Friday,"
Mrs Snitcher said.

When the teams were assigned,
Miles didn't stop tattling.

"Ava is being too loud!"

"Lola won't stop clapping!"

"Jonathan is standing on one foot!"

His team was NOT impressed.

"Miles, hold on a minute," Mrs Snitcher said. "Before we start, let's recite the **TATTLE BATTLE PLEDGE.**"

If a friend is sick, hurt, or in harm's way, then telling someone is OKAY.

And with that, the Tattle Battle
officially began.

Miles knew the rules and he didn't want to let his team down. But sometimes it was hard to know what was tattling and what wasn't.

Mrs Snitcher! Allie is chewing on her pencil!

"Is she sick or hurt or in danger?" Mrs Snitcher asked.

"Well . . . she could choke on it," Miles replied.

"True. But that's not likely."

"Okay," Miles said. "Got it."

Mrs Snitcher!
Emma isn't
wearing socks!

"Is she sick or hurt or in danger?"
Mrs Snitcher asked.

"Well . . . she might
catch a cold," Miles said.

"Maybe. But that's not likely."

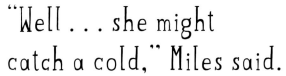

"Okay," Miles said. "Got it."

But he didn't really get it.

He tried hard, but Miles kept letting his team down.
By the end of the week, he found himself alone.

Alone at playtime.

Alone at lunch.

And alone on his walk home.

Nobody wanted to talk to him — especially his teammates. His team was losing the tattle battle and it was all his fault.

"That's it," he said to himself.

"No more tattling. EVER."

That night, Miles was playing in his room when he heard a loud crash. It sounded like it came from the kitchen.

"Hattie, what happened?" Miles asked.

"I wanted another cookie," his sister said. "But when I climbed onto the counter, I slipped."

Miles had a choice to make. Should he tell
his mum or not? He didn't want to be a
tattletale, but Hattie was hurt.

Then Miles remembered the **TATTLE BATTLE** pledge:

If a friend is sick, hurt, or in harm's way, then telling someone is OKAY.

The next day, the class recited the Tattle
Battle pledge right after the first bell.

If a friend is sick, hurt, or in harm's
way, then telling someone is okay.

But at the end of the pledge, Miles McHale went on:

Unless it's sickness, danger, or bullying I see, I will mind my own business and worry about me.

"Miles McHale! That is a wonderful addition to our pledge!" Mrs Snitcher said. "I will take away three tattle points for your team."

Miles **beamed** with pride. His team still lost the Tattle Battle, but that was okay. He apologized to his team and won back his friends.

After that day Miles McHale never tattled
again. In fact, nobody ever tattled again.
Life was perfect.

THE END.